Ostriches

Written by Jo Windsor

CONTENTS

Rigby

Ostriches in the Wild

Ostriches that live in the wild live in the grasslands. They travel in groups of about ten to fifteen birds. Sometimes they travel with zebras and other grass-eating animals. They eat juicy plants, berries and seeds, and insects. Sometimes they will eat rats and reptiles, too.

Did you know . . . ?

• **Ostriches like to drink and bathe in water.**

• **They can go without water for days and days.**

Ostrich Fa

Ostriches are very big birds. They are the largest birds alive on Earth today. If a person (like the adult in the diagram below) stood next to an ostrich, he or she would only come up to the ostrich's shoulders. Some ostriches are over eight feet tall and weigh as much as 345 pounds!

cts and Features

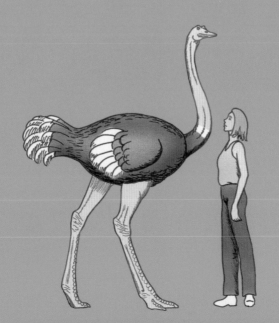

Ostriches are too big to fly. Their wings look like little flaps that carry a fan of fluffy feathers on them. But they have long, strong legs and can run very fast.

Did you know . . . ?

Ostriches can run faster than the fastest human sprinter. They can run as fast as 40 miles per hour to get away from danger.

Keeping Safe

Ostriches see well, too. And because they are tall, they can easily look out for danger from enemies such as lions and cheetahs.

An ostrich is the only bird that has two toes. (Most birds have three or four.) At the end of its toes are long, tough nails. If an ostrich is attacked, it will kick out at its enemy using its nails to defend itself. Under the ostrich's toes are soft pads. These pads stop the ostrich from sinking into the soft sand.

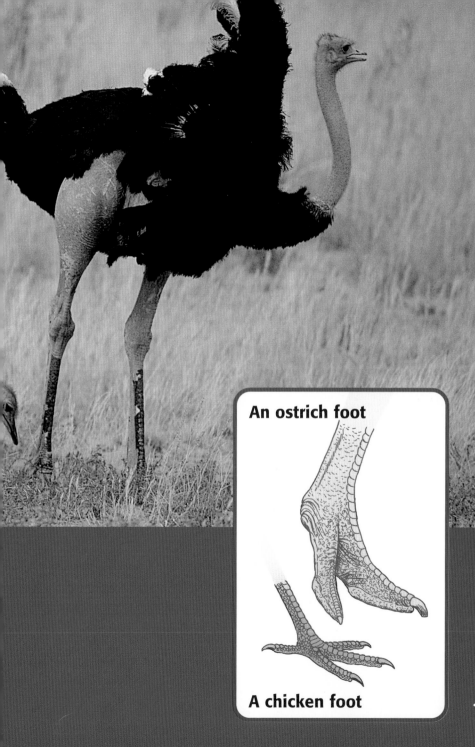

An ostrich foot

A chicken foot

Nests, Eggs, and Chicks

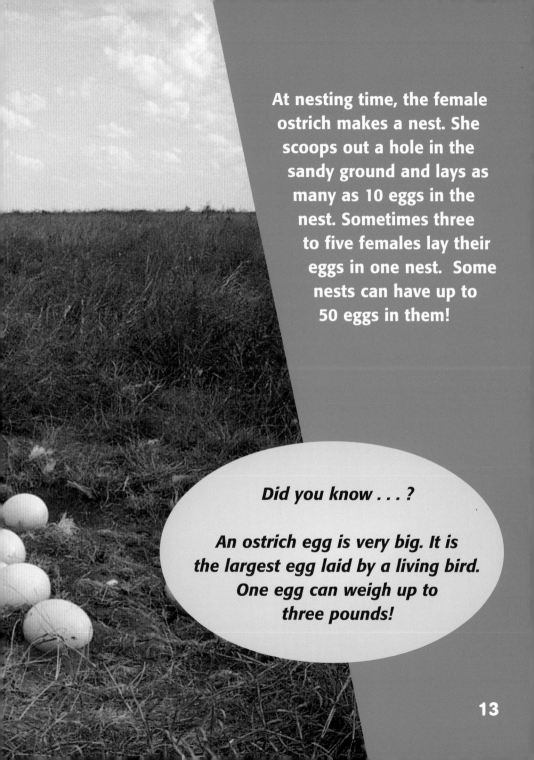

At nesting time, the female ostrich makes a nest. She scoops out a hole in the sandy ground and lays as many as 10 eggs in the nest. Sometimes three to five females lay their eggs in one nest. Some nests can have up to 50 eggs in them!

Did you know . . . ?

An ostrich egg is very big. It is the largest egg laid by a living bird. One egg can weigh up to three pounds!

At night, the male ostrich sits on the eggs. During the day, the female sits on them or sometimes covers them with sand to keep them warm. The eggs take about six weeks to hatch.

The new ostrich chicks are covered with soft feathers called *down*. At about one month old, a young ostrich can run as fast as a fully grown one. Ostriches can live to be 70 years old!

Index

REPORTS record information.

HOW TO WRITE A REPORT:

Step One
- ○ **Choose a topic.**
- ○ **Make a list of the things you know about the topic.**

> **Topic:**
> Ostriches
>
> **What I know:**
> - Ostriches are big birds.
> - Ostriches cannot fly.
> - Ostriches live on grassy plains.

- ○ **Write down the things you need to find out.**

> **What I would like to find out:**
> - Things about where ostriches live
> - How an ostrich makes a nest
> - Other things about ostriches

Reports

Step Two
○ **Find out about the things you need to know. You can:**

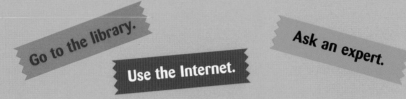

○ **Make notes!**

Step Three
○ **Organize the information. Make some headings.**

Ostrich groups:	How ostriches live:	What ostriches look like:
• Live on sandy plains • Live with other animals – zebra • Live in groups of about 10-15 birds	• Eat berries, plants, insects • Watch out for danger • Can run very fast	• Very tall (can be up to eight feet) • Strong legs • Two toes

Step Four
○ **Use your notes to write your report!**

○ **You can use:**
diagrams, labels, illustrations, photographs, charts, tables, graphs

Guide Notes

Title: Ostriches

Stage: Fluency (1)

Text Form: Informational Report

Approach: Guided Reading

Processes: Thinking Critically, Exploring Language, Processing Information

Written and Visual Focus: Report, Photographs, Index, Captions, Contents Page, Diagrams

THINKING CRITICALLY
(sample questions)
- What do you think this book is going to tell us?
- What do you see on the front cover? What does this tell us about ostriches?
- Focus the children's attention on the contents page. Ask: "What things are you going to find out about in this book?"
- Look at the index. Ask: "What are the things you want to find out about ostriches? What page would you turn to in the book?"
- Why do you think ostriches travel together in groups?
- Why do you think more than one bird lays her eggs in one nest?

EXPLORING LANGUAGE

Terminology
Photograph credits, imprint information, ISBN number, index, contents page

Vocabulary
Clarify: reptiles, sprinter, defend, down
Nouns: chicks, ostrich, bird, wings
Verbs: like, bathe, run, see, kick
Singular/plural: baby/babies, ostrich/ostriches, group/groups, animal/animals

Print Conventions
Apostrophe – possessive (ostrich's toes)